Stains - 2/3/10 am

NAPERVILLE PUBLIC LIBRARIES
Naperville, Illinois

D1278425

Happy Valentine's Day!

Based on the TV series *Little Bill*® created by Bill Cosby as seen on Nick Jr.®

 SIMON SPOTLIGHT
An imprint of Simon & Schuster Children's Publishing Division
1230 Avenue of the Americas, New York, New York 10020
Copyright © 2002 Viacom International Inc. All rights reserved. NICKELODEON, NICK JR., and
all related titles, logos, and characters are trademarks of Viacom International Inc. *Little Bill*
is a trademark of Smiley, Inc.
All rights reserved including the right of reproduction in whole or in part in any form.
SIMON SPOTLIGHT and colophon are registered trademarks of Simon & Schuster.
Manufactured in the United States of America
First Edition   10 9 8 7 6 5 4 3 2 1
ISBN 0-689-84612-6

Happy Valentine's Day!

by Robert Scull

illustrated by Michael Lennicx and Etsu Kahata

Simon Spotlight/Nick Jr.

New York   London   Toronto   Sydney   Singapore

Happy Valentine's Day! We're making cards to give to each other.

Miss Murray says Valentine's Day is the day we tell other people that we love them.

I love you, Miss Murray! You're the best teacher I've ever had!

Happy Valentine's Day, Baby Jamal!
Babies need lots and lots of love and—hey! Let go of my nose!

I love you, Uncle Al! I love you, Aunt Vanessa! I love going to your store after school and eating juice pops with Fuchsia. Slurp! Slurp!

I love you, Fuchsia! You're my cousin, and my friend, too! We take Guppies class together at the pool.

Happy Valentine's Day, Andrew! Remember when we were playing construction in the backyard and we found a real live worm?

Happy Valentine's Day, Kiku! Let's put on a puppet show! You can be the princess, and I'll be the elephant!

Happy Valentine's Day, Monty! Let's play dinosaurs! Rahhrrrr!

I love you, April! You're my favorite big sister!
You taught me how to do a forward roll!

I love you, Mama! You're the best mama in the whole wide world!

I love you, Dad! You make the best Dad's Famous Pizza with the pineapple on it! Superdelicious!

I love you, Alice the Great. You hug me up every day and make me feel safe when I'm scared at night.

I love you, Elephant! You're little and furry, and you make me laugh.

Hey, that was my last Valentine's Day card. Alice the Great says I sure gave out a lot of love today!

Who are all the people that *you* love?